For Mum
J.E.

For Heidi, Chloe & Ben
My Own Loving Family Forever
D.H.

First published in Great Britain in 2007 by Gullane Children's Books
This paperback edition first published in 2008 by

Gullane Children's Books
185 Fleet Street London EC4A 2HS
www.gullanebooks.com

5 7 9 10 8 6 4

Text © Jonathan Emmett 2007
Illustrations © Daniel Howarth 2007

The right of Jonathan Emmett and Daniel Howarth to be identified as the author and illustrator of
this work has been asserted by them in accordance with the Copyright, Designs and Patents Act, 1988.

A CIP record for this title is available from the British Library.

ISBN: 978-1-86233-707-7

Printed and bound in China

I Love You Always and Forever

Jonathan Emmett • Daniel Howarth

GULLANE
CHILDREN'S BOOKS

Longtail and Littletail were playing in the woodland.
They scampered through the bushes and scurried round the trees.

"Catch me if you can!" laughed Littletail.
And she leapt into the long grass.

Littletail was *fast* —
but Longtail was *faster*.
And he caught her up and swept her into his arms.

"You ALWAYS catch me!"
gasped Littletail.
"Do I *always*?" said Longtail.
"Well it won't be *forever*. One day
you will be too fast for
me to catch!"

Littletail wanted to play another game.
"Hide and seek!" she said.
And she bounded off into the brambles.

Longtail counted to a hundred and then went to look.

Littletail was *clever* –
but Longtail was *cleverer*.

And he found her out and caught her by surprise.

"You ALWAYS find me,"
giggled Littletail.
"Do I *always*?" said Longtail.
"Well it won't be *forever*. One
day you will be too clever
for me to find!"

It was getting late,
but Littletail wanted to play one last game.
"Follow the leader!" she said.

And she wriggled down between
the roots of an old tree.
Longtail took a deep breath
and followed after her.

Longtail was *small* —
but Littletail was *smaller*.

And she could squeeze through
where Longtail could not.

"I ALWAYS get through,"
said Littletail proudly.
"Do you *always*?" laughed
Longtail, "Well it won't be
forever, one day you will be
just as big as me!"

Littletail was tired now.
So Longtail carried her home and
laid her down gently in a corner
of their nest.

"I love you, Littletail,"
said Longtail, as he kissed her goodnight.
"You ALWAYS say that," murmured Littletail sleepily.
"Do I *always*?" said Longtail, as he lay down
beside her. "Well that WILL be forever . . ."

"Always and forever," he whispered with a smile.

Other books from Daniel Howarth for you to enjoy . . .

My Special Bedtime Bear
written by Claire Freedman

What makes Little Bear's bedtime so special? Is it a bath, or a story, or a cuddle? It's something else, says Mummy. . . Will Little Bear be able to guess?

For Everyone to Share
written by Gillian Lobel

Little Mouse has never left his nest before and he is thrilled by the sights and sounds outside. But what is this amazing place – and who is it for?

The Cuddliest Cuddle in the World
written by Sarah Nash

Leopard misses Mummy. Can Bear, Python and Monkey help, with a hug or a squeeze or a snuggle? Oh no. There's only one cuddle that's right for Leopard!

Santa's Little Helper
written by Angela McAllister

A big, brown sack seems the perfect place to play hide-and-seek. But Rufus soon finds himself flying through the air . . . on Santa's sleigh!